THE ESCAPE OF MARVIN THE APE

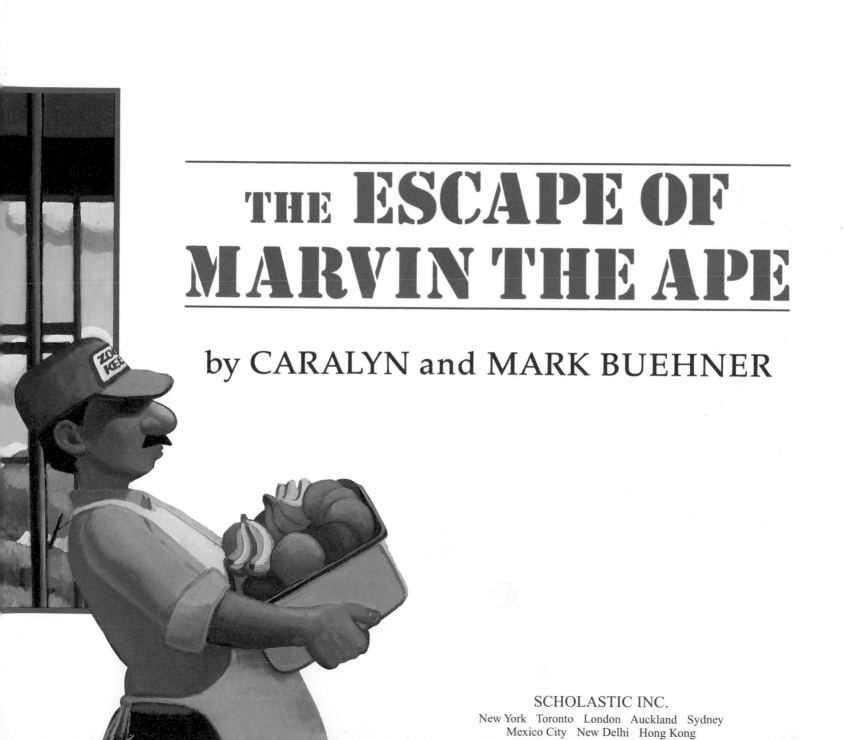

THE ESCAPE OF MARVIN THE APE

by CARALYN and MARK BUEHNER

SCHOLASTIC INC.
New York   Toronto   London   Auckland   Sydney
Mexico City   New Delhi   Hong Kong

It was feeding time, and when the zookeeper wasn't looking, Marvin...

slipped out.

The zookeeper couldn't find Marvin anywhere.

Neither could the police.

Feeling rather hungry, Marvin stopped for a bite.
"Ah, the Jungle Fruit Platter," said the waiter.
"An excellent choice!"

There was a wonderful
park nearby. Marvin
loved to swing.

At the museum Marvin was delighted to find
a painting done by his Uncle Hairy.

The movie mesmerized Marvin.

Marvin fit right in at the toy store.

Marvin loved the ferry. The sea spray was exhilarating!

Marvin found a lot of places to climb.

At a ball game Marvin
caught a pop-up foul.

Marvin was perfectly content with his new life.

Meanwhile, back at the zoo, it was feeding time
and while the zookeeper's head was turned,
Helvetica...

dashed out!

To Heidi, Grant, and Sarah

C. B. and M. B.

ISBN 0-439-249775-5

Text copyright © 1992 by Mark and Caralyn Buehner.
Pictures copyright © 1992 by Mark Buehner.
All rights reserved. Published by Scholastic Inc.,
555 Broadway, New York, NY 10012, by arrangement with Dial Books for Young Readers,
a division of Penguin Books USA Inc. SCHOLASTIC and associated logos are trademarks
and/or registered trademarks of Scholastic Inc.

12 11 10 9 8 7 6 5 4 3 2 1   0 1 2 3 4 5/0

Printed in the U.S.A.   08

First Scholastic Book Fair printing, September 2000

Designed by Mara Nussbaum

The art for this book was prepared by using oil paints over acrylics.
It was then color-separated and reproduced in red, yellow, blue and black halftones.